Children
of the
Clouds

Hollis Lashley

To order additional copies of this book, contact:
Xlibris
1-888-795-4274
www.Xlibris.com
Orders@Xlibris.com

Children
of the
Clouds

Come with me my children as we soar to realms of imagination which can free us from our self inflicted suffering. Come my children as we strap on wings of joy, happiness and laughter; and keep on flying into a place of untold possibilities.

CHILDREN OF THE CLOUDS. AN INTRODUCTION.

When we are born, we are totally dependent on our caregivers for our survival.

The quality of this care giving helps to mold us into who we generally become as adults. Generally, I say, because each individual human being is a unique combination of those behavioral and psychological characteristics which come to define us as a person.

Science has mapped out those ages and stages of development, often rigidly defined by the society in which we happen to be born. Our planet home however, has many and markedly differing abodes. Children exist everywhere with the fundamental need for food, shelter, protection for the body, and of course loving nurturance, which often assumes the last place on the list of needs.

Children everywhere need to be lovingly nurtured, to be cuddled, to be tenderly touched, to be gently and firmly guided into making appropriate behavioral choices, to be listened to, and to have a positive sense of self esteem developed through play and their use of the imagination. Concepts of 'human equality' must flow from the heart, and be recognized in our ability to harness ideas which can serve to unite us as human earthlings, rather than separate us into different races and classes of people.

I believe that the brotherhood and sisterhood of people everywhere, is much more important than the social, idealistic and political divisions practiced by nations and groups.

Each and every one of us I believe, keeps on reliving those lessons we learn in childhood, when we become adults, and often we can't be sure if this happens.

We can learn to be mindful and kind. We can be tolerant and understanding. We can be creatively happy, or stay stuck in our self doubts. We can learn to soar above any kind of circumstance to achieve peace, or we can be tyrannical to our neighbors. Which will you choose?

He would often sit in wonder
Just staring at the sky;
At clouds moving slowly or swiftly,
In processions floating by.
With imagination tickled,
He would watch the clouds and dream:
One day he would be up there
Where so much can be seen.
Those many shapes he visioned,
So many forms were there;
Some said that all this dreaming
Wouldn't get him anywhere.
They called him a cloud watcher.
 They said he was a fool;
But still he kept his watching,
In silence as a rule.

Only one friend believed him,
For somehow she too knew
That clouds were meant for soaring
Beneath the sky so blue.
When he would talk of travel,
Of all there was to see,
She would get all excited,
Joining him in his glee
At one day being airborne
On trails invisible;
Just knowing that believing
Would make it possible.
Oh, how they planned in secret
Adventures they would share;
How they would laugh, triumphantly,
At all who thought them queer.

He envied the birds; those eagles
Flying so free and high,
Always would catch his fancy,
It was magic to his eye.
The free, unfettered gliding,
The diving for their prey;
The strength, the perfect vision,
Their grace in flight each day.
He and his friend would often
Forget about the time,
Until their parents' voices
Would break their mood sublime.
This would be time for running,
Dashing up to their gate;
Time for their evening choring
Before it got too late.

His father would assail him
For dreaming much too much;
But Lisette, his grandmother
Would, with a gentle touch,
Say to him," All is possible
If you really believe,
So don't give up your dreaming,
All things you can achieve.
When the world says that you cannot,
Believe with all your heart;
Things may be slow to happen,
But dare to make a start;
Hold on to your dreams regardless,
Though evidence seems low,
But anything can happen,
True believing makes it so."

He found that he was waiting,
For what, he didn't know.
He often felt excitement,
In sunshine, and in snow.
He felt a strange connection
To everything around:
The stones, the trees, animals,
The stars, flowers, the ground.
At times it seems he could hear
Strange voices in the air;
As though messages were coming
From an unseen somewhere.
But when he told his mother,
She could not understand;
"My son, are you allowing your
Thoughts to get out of hand?"

14

She worried that her boychild,
Whose name was like your own,
Was too imaginative,
His ideas should be outgrown.
But the more that she would tell him
To be real and practical,
The more he saw the magic
In things thought habitual.
Nothing was ordinary
To his way of viewing life.
His peaceful, trusting nature
Could counter any strife.
Though sometimes she got angry,
She would look at her child's face,
With innocence outpouring,
All darkness to erase.

If you are a girl who's reading,
What's the name of his friend?
I will give you several guesses,
Before we reach the end.
What does your mother call you?
I'm sure you love your name,
Well then, you should not worry,
Let us call his friend the same.
Both friends could speak for hours
From deep within their hearts,
About the lightness of being,
And how loving really starts.
What was in the beginning?
What really does ending mean?
What is the soul or spirit?
What lies behind dream scenes?

One day the friends were lying
Beneath a mango tree;
The day was bright and sunny,
Birds chirped with boundless glee.
The wind was cool and blowing
Through leaves of every kind.
Both seem to hear a whisper
Impacting on their mind.
"There is magic in the moment,
There is power in your word,
If you believe sincerely,
All wishes will be heard.
It is time for you to travel,
Prepare to take a ride;
Get on your cloud vehicle,
There are worlds unknown and wide."

One's life is truly magic,

With every possibility,

To do what seems impossible,

To break out and be free,

From every limitation,

From thoughts which keep us down.

There is a mind which serves us

As we choose to smile or frown.

There is magic in each moment,

For deep within every soul,

There is a dynamo for good,

If we but take control.

Whatever thoughts we harness,

Believe we are never wrong,

For one man's tribulation

Is another's victory song.

What happens to us daily
May be important, but
We can respond with power
Or remain in our rut.
It is not our circumstances,
But the way that we respond;
True freedom comes from inside,
Impacting far beyond
Our immediate boundary-
Those whom we often see.
Our every conscious action
Impacts eternity.
The goodness or the thoughtless,
All acts we choose to do,
Sets other acts in motion,
It all comes back to you.

As you think about these questions,
This story must not die,
For in the twinkling of an eye,
Both friends were soaring high.
I am not sure what really happened,
It may be up to you,
Depending on what you believe,
What things you think are true.
Do you believe in magic?
Do you encourage strife?
Do you make peace with others?
Are you in charge of your life?
Are you a loving person?
Do you believe in good?
Do you get mad quite often?
Treat others as you should?

The scene was filled with grandeur,
They saw afar and near;
They spied the tops of houses,
And the raucous village fair.
Rivers shone in the sunshine,
The roads were silvery grey,
Vehicles all seemed toy-sized,
Like those with which we play.
High flying birds were curious,
Not understanding quite,
What were these children doing
Without wings at such a height?
They were both greatly astounded,
By such a sudden shift,
Yet still this new experience
Was providing quite a lift.

They spied the village churches,
The valleys and beyond,
The railroads and the stations,
The old forbidden pond.
They saw the deeper valleys,
The tops of mountains clear.
They saw vast subdivisions,
Repetitively fair.
The gingerbreaded houses,
With curving contoured street,
They saw the farms and playgrounds,
With hues of green, quite neat.
And way out in the distance,
A city could be seen,
With tall erected buildings,
Much brown replacing green.

How could frail clouds support them?
They seemed lighter than air,
Riding so effortlessly,
Their vision crisp and clear.
The clouds formed different patterns,
In shapes to tease their mind,
With variegated shapings
All around and far behind.
They saw large, fairy castles,
Gnomes, aliens, ogres too;
Birds, octopi and insects,
A lady in a shoe.
This was a world of wonder,
Much unlike the one we know;
Beyond imagination,
A mind altering show.

The colors were amazing,
The light was rainbow hued,
Reflecting various angles,
Some perfect, others skewed.
The sun in all its radiance
Blazed with a vibrant light;
The days resplendent glory,
Was holding back the night.
The beauty of this moment,
True, powerful and pure,
Began to overwhelm them;
They could not say for sure
If this was really happening,
Or, was it just a thought?
Was this a part of dreaming,
Which would surely come to nought?

As soon as the questions started ,
And as doubt entered their mind,
Quickly they were both earthbound,
All the glory left behind.
They both looked at each other,
Then quickly the questions flew;
How did you feel, what did you see?
Was this real?, but they knew.
Would anyone believe us,
If we both told them our tale?
Would they think that we are fibbing?
Would all explanations fail?
What do you think my dear reader,
Do you believe or do you doubt?
Can you tell us what you are thinking,
Will you help to figure this out?

Hollis Lashley.

DISCUSSION QUESTIONS!

I hope that you have enjoyed reading 'Children of the Clouds', and that you have been stimulated to explore some of the ideas expressed in the Poem's story.

In an effort to help you to challenge your own thinking and that of others, be it Students, other Book lovers, friends in discussions, or any other individual or group, I have suggested some questions which can follow related Stanzas of the poem. Feel free to design your own questions, discussion topics and overall enquiry as you feel it relates to the story. Thanks for your interest.

The Author.

STANZA 1. PAGE 5

1. Do you enjoy watching clouds? Why or why not?

2. When do you think it best to look at clouds?

3. How would you describe the shapes which you observe in clouds?

STANZA 2. PAGE 7

1. Do you have a best friend with whom you share things?

2. Have you ever traveled , or would like to?

3. What places would you like to visit, and what adventures would you like to enjoy?

STANZA 3. PAGE 9

1. Have you ever seen a live eagle? Describe it.

2. With what kind of birds are you familiar?

3. If you could be a bird, what kind would you choose to be?

STANZA 4. PAGE 11

1. Do you have talks with your parents? What kinds?

2. What ideas do you dream about?

3. Is there anything you are passionate about, and really want to do?

STANZA 5. PAGE 13

1. What daily activities bring you lots of excitement?

2. Do you enjoy walking in the Park, hiking on trails, being near water, looking at flowers, stars, being with nature?

3. Do you prefer to be outdoors or indoors? Explain.

STANZA 6. PAGE 15

1. What is the name of the boy who is mentioned in the story?

2. What kind of person do you think he was?

3. How would you describe his Mother?

STANZA 7. PAGE 17

1. What is the name of the Boy's friend in the story?

2. What sort of things did they speak about?

3. Do you think that they were very good friends? Why or why not?

STANZA 8. PAGE 19

1. What is a mango? Have you seen one? Where?

2. In the story, what was the day like when they were outside? How is your day?

3. Tell us about their experience in your own words.

STANZA 9. PAGE 21

1. How would you describe your own life?

2. How would you like it to be, if you can change it?

3. Tell us about some things you believe, and some you do not.

STANZA 10. PAGE 23

1. What does the word 'Freedom' mean to you?

2. Are you usually happy or unhappy? Why is this so?

3. Who or what do you think is in charge of your life?

STANZA 11. PAGE 25

1. What are some of the questions raised in this stanza?

2. Can you answer any, or can you answer all of them?

3. What do you think happened to the friends?

STANZA 12. PAGE 27

1. Have you ever had a view from up high somewhere?

2. Describe what you saw and how it looked.

3. Why do you think things look smaller from a distance?

STANZA 13. PAGE 29

1. If you were a bird flying above where you live, what would you see?

2. Would you enjoy being a bird? Why or why not?

3. Would you be afraid to travel in a balloon or an airplane?

STANZA 14. PAGE 31

1. Do you believe that you can travel in a cloud? Tell us about it.

2. How do you use your imagination?

3. Tell us about something you have imagined, or make up a story.

STANZA 15. PAGE 33

1. What are your favorite colors?

2. Where do you see your colors the most?

3. Have you ever sees a Sunrise or a Sunset? Describe the colors.

STANZA 16. PAGE 35

1. Do you believe in having adventures?

2. Describe one of your own, or one you would like to have.

3. Tell us one of your stories.

AUTHOR BIO

Hollis Lashley, affectionately called 'Flash' by his acquaintances, holds a graduate degree in Psychology, and is a life-long 'Cultural Activist'. He is a Performance Poet, Singer, Writer, M.C., and has been active in many Multicultural festivals; at The Smithsonian, Strathmore, St. Louis Museum, Minneapolis Institute of Art, Brooklyn Museum, and a host of other venues. He is an avowed student of 'Spirituality', and particularly enjoys the vibrational uplift of sacred space ceremonies, and working with children of all ages. ' I am in awe,' he says, 'of the messages which come through me, from a place of Harmony and Peace. I am eternally thankful for manifesting Love which guides my affairs.' He lives in Maryland with the offspring of his thyme plant, and acknowledges the ' Love of his Life,' who inspires him to be better today than he was yesterday.

ILLUSTRATOR"S BIO

Illustrations for 'Children of the Clouds' were done by Michela Demas, who aspires to become a world renowned Industrial and Product Designer. In High School she has won numerous awards for her Art Work, and is the proud member of the English, Art, and national Honor Societies. She is a Girl Scout Ambassador, a Volunteer for various activities, and is currently a Freshman at the Savannah College of Art and Design. 'Micky', with just a little input from the author, was able to capture the essence of 'Children of the Clouds', and can only move from strength to more strength in her pursuits.

Printed in the United States
By Bookmasters